SPACE BOY

SPACE BOY

Orson Scott Card

Subterranean Press | 2007

First Edition
ISBN: 978-1-59606-111-8

Subterranean Press
PO Box 190106
Burton, MI 48519

SPACE BOY

Todd memorized the Solar System at the age of four. By seven, he knew the distance of every planet from the sun, including the perigee and apogee of Pluto's eccentric orbit, and its degree of declension from the ecliptic. By ten, he had all the constellations and the names of the major stars.

Mostly, though, he had the astronauts and cosmonauts, every one of them, the vehicles they rode in, the missions they accomplished, what years they flew and their ages at the time they went. He knew every kind of satellite in orbit and the distances and orbits that weren't classified and, using the telescope Dad and Mom had given him for his sixth birthday, he was pretty sure he knew 22 separate satellites that were probably some nation's little secret.

He kept a shrine to all the men and women who had died in the space programs, on the launching pad, on landing, or beyond the atmosphere. His noblest heroes were the three Chinese voyagers who had set foot on Mars, but never made it home. He envied them, death and all.

Todd was going into space. He was going to set foot on another planet.

The only problem was that by the time he turned thirteen he knew he was never going to be particularly good at math. Or even *average*. Nor was he the kind of athletic kid who looked like an astronaut. He wasn't skinny, he wasn't fat, he was just kind of soft-bodied with slackish arms no matter how much he exercised. He ran to school every day, his backpack bumping on his back. He got bruises on his butt, but he didn't get any faster.

When he ran competitively in P.E. he was always one of the last kids back to the coach, and he couldn't ever tell where the ball was coming when they threw to him, or, when it left his own hand, where it was likely to go. He wasn't the last kid chosen for teams—not while Sol and Vawn were in his P.E. class. But no

one thought of him as much of a prize, either.

But he didn't give up. He spent an hour a day in the back yard throwing a baseball against the pitch-back net. A lot of the time, the ball missed the frame altogether, and sometimes it didn't reach the thing at all, dribbling across the lawn.

"If I had been responsible for the evolution of the human race," he said to his father once, "all the rabbits would have been safe from my thrown stones and we would have starved. And the sabertooth tigers would have outrun whoever didn't starve."

Father only laughed and said, "Evolution needs every kind of body. No one kind is best."

Todd wouldn't be assuaged so easily. "If the human race was like *me*, then launching rockets and going into space would have to wait for the possums to do it."

"Well," said Father, "that would mean smaller spaceships and less fuel. But where in a spacesuit would they stow that tail?"

Really funny, Dad. Downright amusing. I actually thought about smiling.

He couldn't tell anybody how desperate and sad he was about the fact that he would probably have to become a high school drama teacher like his dad. Because if he *did* say how he felt, they'd make him go to a shrink again to deal with his "depression" or his "resentment of his father" the way they did after his mother disappeared when he was nine and Dad gave up on searching for her.

The shrink just wouldn't accept it when he screamed at him and said, "My mother's gone and we don't know where she went and everybody's stopped looking! I'm not depressed, you moron, I'm *sad*. I'm *pissed off!*"

To which the shrink replied with questions like, "Do you feel better when you get to call a grownup a 'moron' and say words like 'pissed'?" Or, worse yet, "I think we're beginning to make progress." Yeah, I didn't choke you for saying that, so I guess that's progress.

Nobody even remembered these days that sometimes people were just plain miserable because something really bad was going on in their lives and they didn't need a drug, they needed somebody to say, "Let's go get your mother now, she's ready to come home," or, "That was a great throw—look, after all these years, Todd's become a *terrific* pitcher and he's great at math so let's make him an astronaut!"

Ha ha, like that would ever happen.

Instead, he took a kitchen timer with him out to the back yard every afternoon, and when it went off he'd drop what he was doing and go inside and fix dinner. Jared kept trying to help, which was okay because Jared wasn't a complete idiot even though he was only seven and certifiably insane. Todd's arm was usually pretty sore from misthrowing the ball, so Jared would take his turn stirring things.

There was a lot of stirring, because when Todd cooked, he *cooked*. Okay, he mostly opened soup cans or cans of beans or made mac and cheese, but he didn't nuke them, he made them on the stove. He told Dad that it was because he liked the taste better when it was cooked that way, but one day when Jared said, "Mom always cooked on the stove," Todd realized that's why he liked to do it that way. Because Mom knew what was right.

It wasn't *all* soup or beans or macaroni. He'd make spaghetti starting with dry noodles and plain tomato sauce and hamburger in a frying pan, and Dad said it was great. Todd even made the birthday cakes for all their birthdays, including his own, and for the last few years he made them from recipes, not from mixes. Ditto with his chocolate chip cookies.

Why was it he could calculate a half recipe

involving thirds of a cup, and couldn't find n in the equation $n=5$?

He took a kind of weird pleasure from the way Dad's face got when he bit into one of Todd's cookies, because Todd had finally remembered or figured out all the things Mom used to do to make her cookies different from other people's. So when Dad got all melancholy and looked out the window or closed his eyes while he chewed, Todd knew he was thinking about her and missing her even though Dad *never* talked about her. I made you remember her, Todd said silently. I win.

Jared didn't talk about Mom, but that was for a different reason. For a year after Mom left, Jared talked about her all the time. He would tell everybody that the monster in his closet ate her. At first people looked at him with fond indulgence. Later, they recoiled and changed the subject.

He only stopped after Dad finally yelled at him. "There's no monster in your closet!" It sounded like somebody had torn the words from him like pulling off a finger.

Todd had been doing the dishes while Dad put Jared to bed, and by the time Todd got to the back of the house, Jared was in his room crying and Dad was sitting on the edge of his and Mom's bed and *he* was crying and then Todd, like a complete fool, said, "And you send *me* to a shrink?"

Dad looked up at Todd with his face so twisted with pain that Todd could hardly recognize him, and then he buried his face in his hands again, and so Todd went in to Jared and put his arm around him and said, "You've got to stop saying that, Jared."

"But it's true," Jared said. "I saw her go. I warned her but she did the very exact thing I told her *not* to do because it almost got my arm the time I did it, and—"

Todd hugged him closer, "Right, I know, Jared. I know. But stop saying it, okay? Because nobody's ever going to believe it."

"You believe me, don't you, Todd?"

Todd said, "Of course I do. Where else could she have gone?" Why not agree with the crazy kid? Todd was already seeing a shrink. He had nothing to lose. "But if we talk about it, they'll just think we're insane. And it made Dad cry."

"Well he made *me* cry too!"

"So you're even. But don't do it anymore, Jared. It's a secret."

"Same thing with the monster's elf?"

"The monster itself? What do you mean?"

"The elf. Of the monster. I can't talk about the elf?"

Geeze louise, doesn't he let up? "Same thing with the monster's elf and his fairies and his dentist, too."

Jared looked at him like he was insane. "The monster doesn't have a dentist. And there's no such thing as fairies."

Oh, right, lecture *me* on what's real and what's not!

So it went on, days and weeks and months, Todd fixing dinner and Dad getting home from after-school play practices and they'd sit down and eat and Dad would tell funny things that happened that day, doing all the voices. Sometimes he *sang* the stories, even when he had to have thirty words on the same note till he came up with a rhyme. They'd all laugh and it was great, they had a great life…

Except Mom wasn't there to sing harmony. The way they *used* to do it was they'd take turns singing a line and the other one would rhyme to it. Mom could always make a great rhyme that was exactly in rhythm with the song. Dad was funny about it, but Mom was actually *good*.

Grief is like that. You live on, day to day, happy sometimes, but you can always think of something that makes you sad all over again.

Everybody had their secrets, even though everybody else knew them. Jared had his closet monster *and* its elf. Dad had his memory of Mom, which he never discussed with anyone. Todd had his secret dreams of going to other worlds.

Then on a cool Saturday morning in September, a few weeks after his thirteenth birthday, he was out in the side yard, screwing the spare hose onto the faucet so he could water Mom's roses, when he heard a hissing sound behind him and turned around in time to see a weird kind of shimmering appear in midair just a few feet out from the wall.

Then a bare child-size foot slid from nowhere into existence right in the middle of the shimmering.

If it had been a hairy claw or some slime-covered talon or the mandibles of some enormous insect, Todd might have been more alarmed. Instead, his fear at the strangeness of a midair arrival was trumped by his curiosity. All at once Jared's talk about Mother disappearing in the closet because she did the same thing *he* did when the monster "caught his arm" didn't sound quite as crazy.

The foot was followed, in the natural course of things, by a leg, with another foot snaking out beside it. The legs were bare and kept on being bare right up to the top, where Todd was vaguely disgusted to see that whoever was coming was *not* a child. It was a man as hairy as the most apelike of the guys in gym class, and as sweaty and naked as they were when they headed for the showers. Except that he was about half their size.

"Eew, get some pants on," said Todd, more by reflex than anything. Since the little man's head had not yet emerged, Todd didn't feel like he was being rude to a person—personhood really seemed to require a head, in Todd's opinion—but apparently the dwarf—no, the *elf*, it was pretty obvious that Jared must have been referring to something like this— must have heard him somehow because he stopped wriggling further out, and instead a hand snaked out of the opening and covered the naked crotch.

The elf must have been holding on to something on the other side of that opening, because all of a sudden, instead of wriggling further out, he simply dropped the rest of the way, hit the ground, and rolled. It reminded Todd of the way a pooping dog will strain and strain, making very little progress, and then all of a sudden the poop breaks off and drops. He knew it was a disgusting thought, which made him regret that there was no one there to say it to.

Still, he couldn't help laughing, especially because this particular dropping was a stark naked man about half Todd's size.

At the sound of Todd's laughter, the man rolled over and, now making no attempt at modesty, said, "Oh, it's you."

"Why, have we met?" asked Todd. "What are you doing naked in my back yard? I think that's illegal."

"In case you weren't watching," said the man, "I just squeezed through the worm, so it's not like any clothes I was wearing would have made it anyway. And what are you doing out here? You're never out here."

"I'm out here all the time," said Todd.

The elf pointed to the back yard, around the corner of the house. "You're always over there, throwing a ball at a fishnet. I admit I wondered why you haven't figured out that the net will *never* catch the ball."

"Who are you, and what are you doing here, and why did Jared know about you and the rest of us didn't, and where is my mother, what happened to her?"

"Do you mind if I get dressed first?"

"Yes, I do mind." If this was Todd's only chance to get his questions answered, he wasn't going to be put off. If the stories about elves and leprechauns were true—and now he had to figure they must have *some* basis in fact—they were tricky and dishonest and you couldn't take any of them at their word. Which meant that they would fit right into eighth grade. Todd was experienced at being suspicious.

"Too bad," said the elf.

The elf started walking toward the fence that separated the side yard from the front yard. Todd got in front of him to block his way.

The elf swatted him away. It *looked* like a swat, anyway—but it felt like the back of his hand sank two inches into Todd's shoulder and shoved him out of the way with all the force of a bulldozer. He smacked into the bricks of the side of the house, and slid sharply enough that his arm was scraped raw. His head also rang from the impact, and when he reached up his sore arm to touch his face, the right side of his forehead up near the hairline was bleeding.

"Hey!" Todd yelled at him. "You got no right to do that! That *hurt!*"

"Boo-hoo, poor baby," said the elf. He was kneeling now. It seemed he counted boards in the fence and then plunged his hand right down into the dirt in front of a certain board.

Todd had dug in this hard-clay soil. It was hard enough to dig when the soil was wet; when it was dry, it was like trying to dig a hole in the bottom of a dish using only a spoon. But the little man's hand plunged in as if the dirt were nothing but Jell-O and Todd began to realize that just because somebody was little didn't mean he wasn't strong.

The elf's hand came up with a metal strongbox. He punched buttons to do the combination of the lock, and then lifted it open. Inside were clothes in a plastic bag. Within a minute, the man had pants and a shirt on. They looked like they had been bought at Gap Kids—new enough but way too cute for a guy as hairy as this.

"Where did you get those shoes?" asked Todd. They were like clown shoes, much wider and longer than his feet. Almost like snowshoes.

"I had them specially made," the elf said irritably.

For the first time, Todd realized that despite the elf's fluency, he had an accent—English wasn't his native language. "Where are you from?" he asked.

"Oh, right, like you'd recognize the name," said the elf.

"I mean is it another country? Or…" Todd looked at the shimmering in the air, which was

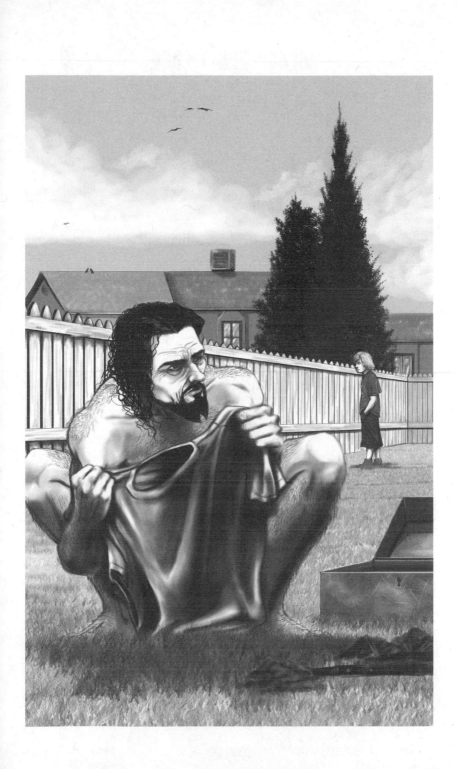

now *way* less visible and fading fast. "Like, another dimension?"

"Another planet," said the elf. "And your mouth can't make the sounds necessary to pronounce the real name. But your mother calls it 'Lilliput.'"

"My mother?" said Todd. All at once it felt like his heart was in his throat. "She's alive, like Jared said?"

"Of course she's alive, why wouldn't she be alive? I warned Jared about the worm and he warned your mother, but did she *believe* him? No, he was just a child, so now she's stuck there and she's starting to get annoyed about it."

"Starting? She's been gone four years."

"Time doesn't work the same way back home. Your mother's only been gone for about a week."

"Four years!" shouted Todd. "She's been gone four years and why hasn't she come home? If *you* can get here, why can't she?"

"Because she's too big to get where she needs to go," said the elf. "You think I'm small, but I'm a tall man in my world. Your mother—she's a giant. Only she's a big *weak* giant. A big weak naked giant because clothes don't do so well coming through the worm—"

"What worm? Where's the worm?"

The elf waved toward the shimmering in the air. "That's the worm's anus. The mouth is in the closet in Jared's bedroom."

"So there really is a monster there."

"Not a monster," said the elf. "A worm. It's not out to get anybody. It just sucks stuff in at one end of a connection between worlds. You'd be surprised how much energy is released where worlds connect, if you can bridge them, and worms can do it, so they attach the two worlds together and process things through. Like earthworms. Only worldworms don't move, they just sit there and suck."

"Suck *what?*" said Todd.

"I told you, energy. They suck a star's worth of energy in a year."

"Out of Jared's *closet?*"

"No." The elf sounded scornful. "Out of the friction between universes. The differing time flows—they rub up against each other because they aren't synchronized. Four years for you, a week for your mother—you think that timeflow difference doesn't *burn?*"

"Don't talk to me like I'm an idiot," said Todd. "How exactly was I supposed to know any of this?

I didn't even know your universe existed."

"Your mother disappears and you don't *suspect* something?"

"Yeah, we suspected that somebody pointed a gun at her and made her go with them. Or she maybe ran away from us because she stopped loving Dad. Or she died in some freak accident and her body simply hasn't been found. But no, the idea of her disappearing into another universe with a different timeflow didn't come up much."

"I *heard* Jared tell your father."

"Jared told Dad about a monster in the closet! For pete's sake, if I hadn't seen you come out of midair myself I wouldn't believe it. What, are little kids taught all about the friction between timeflows in *your* world?"

The elf looked a little abashed. "Actually, no," he said. "In fact, I'm the scientist who finally figured out what's going on. I've been coming back and forth between worlds, riding the worm for years. Not just here, either, this is the fourth worm I've ridden."

"So you're like—what, the Einstein of the elves?"

"More like Galileo. Nobody believes me on my end of the worm, either. In fact, most of my science and math come from your world. Which is why I expected it to be obvious to *you*."

"Just because I'm from planet Earth I'm supposed to be a math genius? I guess that means that since you're an elf, you make great shoes. You probably made those stupid clown shoes yourself."

The elf glowered at him. "I'm not an elf. And I don't make shoes. I don't *wear* shoes back home. I wear them here because unless I wear shoes with wide soles to spread my weight, I sink too far into the ground, which slows me down and leaves tracks everywhere."

"They make you look stupid."

"I'd look a lot stupider up to my ankles in asphalt."

While they'd been talking, Todd had also been thinking. "You said Mom's been gone for only a week."

"The timeflow difference fluctuates, but that's about right."

"So she hasn't even begun to miss me yet. Us. Yet."

"She's a big baby about it. Cries all the time. Worse than your father."

Todd remembered hearing his father cry, how private that had been. "You spy on us?"

"The worm I'm riding comes out here, and to get home I have to go into your brother's bedroom. I'm not spying, I'm traveling. With my eyes and ears open." The elf sighed. "OK, so I stop and gather data.

I'm a scientist. You're an interesting people. And you'll notice I called you *people*, not some insulting diminutive derogatory name like 'elves.'"

"If Mom could fit through the hole going the other way, she can fit through to come home."

The elf—for lack of a better name—did a weird move with his fingers. He'd done it a couple of times before, and Todd finally realized that where he came from, it must be the equivalent of rolling his eyes. "Like I said, in my world she's huge. And very…light. Insubstantial. She can't *do* anything. She can barely make her voice heard."

Todd tried to imagine what that might mean. "She's some kind of mist?"

The elf chuckled. "Yes, she has some fog-like properties."

Todd took a threatening step toward him. "Don't laugh at my mother!"

"If you'd seen her during a windstorm, trying to hold on to trees, *anything* to keep from blowing away—"

"It's not funny!" Todd tried to shove him, but it was like hitting a brick wall. It hurt his hands, and the elf didn't even budge.

"You still don't get it," said the elf. "I'm very dense."

"It too a moment for Todd to realize he meant

dense like in physics instead of *dense* as in "kind of dumb."

"I want my mother back. And you're a lousy sack of crap to make fun of her when she's stuck in your world."

"Oh, and you didn't make fun of *me* at *all*, I take it," said the elf. "When I popped through naked, that wasn't funny to you?"

"It was disgusting. And if Mother could fit through the wormhole in the closet, she must have fit through the worm's…whatever, on *your* side. So she *can* fit."

"Anus," said the elf. "The worm's mouth is in your closet. Its anus, in my world, is on a lovely wooded hillside behind my house. And yes, it has a mouth and an anus on both worlds. It's a single organism, but its digestive systems are bidirectional. It eats both worlds at once."

"Eats *what?*" Now Jared's childhood fears of being eaten by the monster in the closet seemed too literally true.

"Eats time. Eats dark matter. Eats dust. I have no idea. Why does gravity suck? I'm just starting to try to figure out a whole branch of science that neither your world nor mine knows anything about."

Todd's mind jumped back to the real question. "My mother lives with you?"

"Your mother is living in the woods because there's more room for her there and she can avoid being seen. She can avoid having someone maliciously dissipate her."

"What?"

"Throw rocks at her, for instance, until she's so full of holes she can't stick together and the bits of her just drift away."

"What kind of sick people *are* you in that world!"

"She's a huge woman who looks as translucent as mist! The few who have met her don't think she's alive! *They* haven't been to this world. They're ignorant peasants, most of them. It's all very awkward." The elf leaned in close to Todd. "I'm doing everything I can to set things right. But please remember that I didn't take her to my world. She did that herself in spite of being warned. And I didn't put that stupid worm's mouth in your closet."

Then he got a strange look on his face. "Well, actually, I did, but not deliberately."

"You *put* it there?"

"The worm is apparently drawn to inhabited places. I don't know what it thinks we are, or if it thinks at all, but I've never seen a worm that wasn't close to the dwelling place of a sentient being. It may even be drawn to people who might want to use it to travel from world to world. It might have been aware of my passion for exploration, which is why the anus showed up in my front garden." Then, almost to himself: "Though it would have been much more convenient to have the *mouth* within easy reach."

"My mother didn't want to travel anywhere," said Todd. As he was saying it, he realized that maybe it wasn't Mother or even Jared who had drawn the worm to Jared's closet. There *was* someone in their family who had a passionate desire to travel to other planets.

"Your brother kept putting things through the worm," said the elf. "I'd find them in my garden. Wooden blocks. Socks. Underwear. A baseball cap. Little model cars. Plastic soldiers. A coat hanger. Money. And once a huge, misty, terrified cat."

Todd thought back to all the times things had disappeared. His favorite plastic soldiers. His baseball cap. His socks. His underwear. His Hot Wheels cars. Jared must have been stealing them to make them disappear down the wormhole. He had no idea where Jared got the cat, but it would have been just like him.

Of course, maybe Jared thought he was *feeding* the monster in the closet. Placating it, so it wouldn't come out of the closet and eat him. Was this how the worship of idols began? You put things in a certain place and they disappear into thin air—what could you imagine, except it was a hungry god?

And the kid was smart enough to figure out that if he needed to make stuff disappear, it might as well be something of Todd's. Amoral little dork.

"The first time I saw something appear in midair," said the elf, "it was broad daylight. I knew what it was—I'd been investigating worms for some time. It was a…hobby of mine. But I also knew that if people found out I had one in our neighborhood, I'd either be inundated with curiosity seekers, or plagued by pious people determined to sit around and see what the gods would give them, or I'd be arrested for witchcraft."

"Witchcraft? That's just superstition."

"Don't get superior with me. I've been studying your culture for years. On television you marry witches, but in real life you burn them. And if somebody in your world saw *me* plop out of the sky…"

"Which I just did."

"…then what do you think would happen *here?*"

"Scientists would come and study the worm and—"

"You really are naive. No self-respecting scientist would come anywhere near something like this, because it would sound like pure tabloid journalism. They could lose their careers!"

"Is that what happened to you?" asked Todd. "Have you lost your career?"

"I don't have a career, exactly."

"You're not a scientist?"

"In our world, scientists are rare and they work alone."

Todd gave that the worst possible spin. "People think you're crazy and pay no attention to you."

"They'd think I was crazy and pay a *lot* of attention to me if I hadn't moved the anus."

It occurred to Todd that "moving the anus" could be rendered as "hauling ass," which he found amusing.

"Now look who's laughing," said the elf.

Todd got back to business. "You can *move* this thing."

"With enormous difficulty and great risk."

"So you could move it out of our closet. You didn't have to put it there!"

"I didn't put it in your closet. I moved it a hundred

yards to a dense woods behind my house. I had no idea where it would go in *your* world. It moved a thousand miles. I couldn't plan its location here, and I'm not going to change it now. It happens to be well-hidden and convenient to a town with a decent library. It's perfect."

"Perfect for you. Really lousy for my mother and our whole family."

"I told you, that was not my fault." The elf sounded bored, which made Todd mad.

"Listen, you little runt, you get my mother back and then you get your worm out of our house and out of my yard!"

The elf was just as furious. "Listen yourself, you bug of a boy, don't give orders to a 'runt' who happens to be dense enough that I could reach into your chest with my bare hand and pull out your beating heart and stuff it into the worm's anus! You have 'suppository' written all over you."

There was a moment of silence while Todd realized that the elf was right. There was nothing Todd could do to threaten him; so it did no good to get angry or make demands. If he was going to get any help from the elf, he'd have to keep the conversation calm. So he said the first non-threatening thing he could think of. "That's like what they did in *Temple of Doom*."

Exasperated, the elf said, "*What* is what *who* did? And where is the temple of doom?"

"It's a movie. An Indiana Jones movie. They pulled the beating heart out of their sacrificial victims."

"I don't have time to go to movies," said the elf. "I don't have time to talk to ignorant, pugnacious boys."

"What does pugnacious even mean?"

"It means that I apparently have become much more fluent in your ridiculously misspelled and underinflected language than you will ever be."

"Well, you're a scientist and I'm not." And then something else dawned on Todd. If the worm had been attracted to Todd, then it must also have been attracted to this guy and for maybe the same reason. "You're a space traveler."

"No I'm not."

"You travel between worlds."

"But not through space. My world doesn't exist in your space. No light from our sun can ever possibly reach this planet. You cannot board any kind of imaginable spacecraft and get from there to here no matter how long you flew. I am not a space traveler."

"You get from one planet to another. And you didn't have to build anything or get good grades in any subject or anything at all. It was just dumb luck, but you got to visit an alien world!"

"From your tone of voice, I suspect you're about to say, 'No fair'!"

"Well, why should *you* get to do it, and I can't!"

"Oh, you can—if you're stupid enough to reach into the throat of the worm and get sucked through and pooped out into a world where you're like a kind of atmospheric diarrhea."

"So what does that make you, interplanetary constipation or something?"

"It makes me sick of talking to you. I've got work to accomplish." The elf started walking away.

"Hey!" called Todd.

The elf didn't pause.

"What's your name!" Todd yelled.

The elf turned around. "You don't need my name!"

Why not? Did it give Todd some kind of magical power? Todd remembered a fairy tale about secret names that his mother used to read to them. "Then I'll call you Rumpelstiltskin!"

To his surprise, the elf came back, looking very angry. "What did you call me?"

"Rumpelstilskin?" said Todd, remembering the heart-grabbing threat.

"Don't you ever call me that again."

Which almost made Todd call him that twenty times in a row. But no, he had to have this guy's cooperation if he was going to get his mother back. "Then tell me your name."

The elf stood there, irritably considering. "Eggo," he finally said.

Of all things. "Like the waffles?"

"Like *me*. My *name* is Eggo. And yes, your mother already explained about frozen toaster waffles. In my language it doesn't mean anything of the kind."

"What *does* it mean?"

"It means me, I told you! Just like Todd means you. It's a name, not a word."

The elf—Eggo—turned around and headed out across the back yard. Todd almost laughed, his gait was so ducklike as he swung those big shoes around each other so he didn't trip on his own feet. But it wasn't funny. Eggo was doing what he had to in order not to sink into the earth; what was Mother doing, to keep from dissolving into mist on the other side?

Todd went back into the house, determined to

do something. He didn't know what, yet, but he had to act, stir things up, change things so that somehow Mom would come back and life would get back to normal. Or maybe it would get even worse, maybe people would die, but isn't that what they already believed happened to Mom? They'd already been through a death and now there was a chance to undo it.

And Todd knew that it was going to be him who did the undoing. Not because he was the smartest or strongest one in the family but because he had decided to. Because he was going to go through the worm and get Mom home. He was going to travel to another world. It's what he was born for.

He couldn't say that to anybody or they'd think he was crazy.

Not like seeing elves materialize in the back yard...

Dad was still asleep, as usual on a Saturday morning. Jared was up, but he hadn't left his room yet. Todd went in and sat beside the little sorted-out piles of Legos that Jared was drawing from to build his...what?

"It's like an amusement park ride," said Jared.

"It looks like a skyscraper."

"I put little Lego guys into this hole at the top and they bounce around inside and pop out here."

"That's not an amusement park, it's a machine for killing people."

"It's not for killing people," Jared said vehemently—but quietly, so Dad wouldn't wake up. "People are perfectly OK when they come through the other side. They are *alive*."

He's building the stupid worm, thought Todd. "You're right," said Todd. "They're perfectly all right when they come out the other end."

Jared looked up at him suspiciously.

"I met your elf," said Todd.

"There's no elf," said Jared.

"All my stuff you put through the mouth in the closet," said Todd. "By the way, thanks for stealing my Hot Wheels and all my other crap."

"I didn't steal anything."

"Mother's alive," said Todd. "I know it now."

But Jared didn't look relieved or happy or anything. In fact, he looked panicky. Only when Todd felt a strong hand on his shoulder did he realize that Dad must have come into the room and heard him.

Dad had never handled Todd roughly before, not like this. The grip on his shoulder was harsh—it hurt.

And he dragged Todd so quickly out of the room that he could barely keep his feet under him. "Hey!" Todd yelled. "Hey, hey, what're you—"

But by then they were in Dad's room and the door slammed shut behind them. "What the *hell* do you think you're doing?" said Dad. He practically threw Todd onto the bed. Then he leaned over him, one hand on either side of him, his face angry and only about a foot away from Todd's. "Do you think it's funny to try to make your brother believe that all his childhood fantasies are true?"

"Dad," said Todd.

"It's all a joke to you, is that it?" Dad said, his voice a harsh whisper. "All that I've done, trying to make life normal again, you think it's really clever to undo it and make your brother think that your mother is still alive somewhere. Do you know what that would mean? That your mother *wants* to be away from us, that she *chose* to leave us like that. You think that's *better* than believing she's dead? Well you're wrong."

"It's not about believing anything," said Todd quietly, reasonably, trying to calm Father down.

And it worked, at least a little. Dad stopped looming over him and sat on the bed beside him.

"What is it, then, Todd? Why are you telling your brother that he should believe his mother is alive?"

"Because she is, Dad," said Todd.

Dad turned away from him, slumped over, leaning on his knees. "It never ends."

"Dad," said Todd, "I didn't believe it either. I thought she was dead until this very exact morning when I found out the truth. Something I saw with my own eyes. Dad, I'm not crazy and I'm not joking."

Dad was now leaning his forehead on his hands. "What do you think crazy people say, Todd?"

"They say there's a worm that passes between two worlds, and the mouth of it is in Jared's closet and it sucks things out of our world and drops them into another. And Mother's there, only she can't get back because the rules of physics are different in that place, and she's not as dense as we are here, so she can't hold onto things and she doesn't know how to find the mouth on the other side and the jerk who's studying the thing, the guy who moved the mouth of the worm into Jared's closet, he doesn't care about anything except his stupid science. And I can't go there myself and get Mom back if you don't help."

By the time Todd was through, Dad had sat up

and was staring at him. "Yes, Todd," he finally said. "That's exactly what crazy people say."

"But I can prove it," said Todd.

Dad buried his face in his hands again. "God help us," he murmured.

"Dad, what if there's one chance in a million that I'm not crazy. Do you love me enough to give me that chance? Will you come and *look?*"

Dad nodded behind his hands. "Yeah, I'll look." He stood up. "Show me whatever you've got to show me, Todd."

Todd knew perfectly well that Dad still thought he was crazy. But he was at least willing to give him a chance. So Todd led the way back into Jared's room.

Jared was sitting on his bed, pressed into the corner of the room, holding a little Lego guy in one hand and gnawing on a finger. Not the nail, the whole finger in his mouth, chewing on it like it was gum.

"Get your hand out of your mouth, Jared, and come over here and help me," said Todd.

Jared didn't move.

"I've got to show Dad the worm's mouth," said Todd. "And you're the one who knows exactly where it is."

Jared didn't move.

"I can't believe you'd do this, Todd," said Dad. His voice was full of grief. "Jared's made so much progress, and now look."

"Listen to me, both of you! Mom's still alive on the other end of this thing! Stop trying to solve things, Dad, stop trying to make sense of it and just *watch*."

Todd picked up Jared's Lego thing, his representation of the worm, and took it to the closet and flung open the door.

He couldn't see anything at all like that slice of air out in the back yard. He walked back and forth in front of the closet, trying to get the right angle. Then he went to the drapes and opened them, letting sunlight flood in. It didn't help.

"Todd," said Dad.

"Jared," said Todd angrily, "if you don't help me, Dad's going to think we're both crazy and we'll *never* get Mom back. Now get off your butt and help me find it!"

Jared didn't move.

Todd took the Lego thing and stepped right into the closet and began waving his hand around, thrusting here and there, trying to accidentally find the hole in the air.

"Stop it," said Jared.

"What do you care whether I fall in or not?" said Todd. "Of course, if you guys aren't helping, I'll fall through just like Mom did, and I'll be just as helpless as she is on the other side, and then you'll lose us both, but at least Dad will know I'm not crazy!" Todd stopped and looked at his father. "Only now things will get really ugly, because the cops will want to know what happened to your son Todd, and they'll begin to get curious about how *two* people from the same family both disappeared under mysterious circumstances. I watch *Law & Order*, Dad. You'll be the prime suspect. And then they'll think *you're* crazy, unless *you* fall through the hole to prove it to them. And then Jared will be an orphan and there'll be some cops who are thrown out of the police force because they insist that they saw this man—this mass murder suspect—disappear into thin air in his son's closet. Is that how you want this to go?"

Father was looking halfway between grief-stricken and terrified. But Jared had gotten off his bed and was padding across the floor, stepping over Lego piles. He took the Lego structure out of Todd's hands. Todd let him.

"Give me something," said Jared.

"Like what?"

"Your shoe."

"Why can't you use something of your own for once?" said Todd.

"I can't use my own stuff, because then it grabs hold of my hand and sucks me in."

"You mean it knows who *owns* things?"

"When I throw your crap in it doesn't grab my hand," said Jared.

"Then let *me* throw *your* crap in."

"Do you want Dad to see this or not?" demanded Jared.

Todd peeled his shoe off, but he didn't give it to Jared. "Shoes are expensive, in case you didn't know," he said. He rolled his dirty white sock off. "Socks are cheap."

"They also stink," said Jared. "You're such a pig, you never wash your clothes, you just wear them forever." But he took the sock and ducked into the closet—ducked *under* something—and then shoved Todd out. "Both of you watch," he said.

Then he held the sock out between his fingers and began swinging it back and forth like a floppy pendulum.

And then, on one of the outward swings, it

stopped and didn't come back. It just hung there in the air, Jared holding onto the top of the sock, and something else holding onto the toe end.

"Now it's got it," said Jared. "Watch close because it's quick."

Jared let go. The sock disappeared.

But Todd had indeed been watching closely, and even though it happened fast, he saw that the sock was sucked into something by the toe.

Jared was pressed up against the closet door frame. He was still scared of the thing. Smart kid.

"Get out of the closet, Jared," said Dad. His voice was soft. He was scared, too.

Jared sidled out.

Dad looked from Jared to Todd, back and forth. Then he settled on Todd. "Why didn't you tell me before?"

"Because up till this morning I thought the kid was wacked out."

"Thanks," said Jared.

"You mean you never saw him do this?" said Dad.

"Did it look like I knew where the thing was?" asked Todd.

"I've put things in that closet hundreds of times," said Dad.

"You have to come at it from the side," said Jared. "And kind of slow."

"And Mother did that?"

"She was trying to prove to me that there was nothing there. I told her how it worked, and so she was going to prove to me that it was just a nightmare. I begged her not to do it. I cried, I screamed at her, I threw things at her to get her to stop."

"Jared," said Dad, "that would just convince her that it was all the more important to prove it to you."

"It got her," said Jared. "I tried to pull her back but it got her whole arm and shoulder and her head so she couldn't even talk to me and then it just grabbed the rest of her, all at once, and ripped her leg right out of my hands." Jared was crying now. "I told you and told you but you didn't believe me and Todd finally said to stop talking about it because you'd think I was crazy."

Dad held Jared against him, patting his shoulder, letting him have his cry. He looked at Todd. "What happened this morning? What convinced you that it was real?"

So Todd told Dad all about Eggo the superdense scientist elf with duckfoot shoes, which sounded crazier the more he talked. He had to keep stopping and reminding Dad about the sock that disappeared, and half the time he was really reminding himself that this insane thing was real.

"I don't know what to make of all this," said Dad. "I don't know what to do. We can't tell this to the cops."

"We *could*," said Todd. "We could demonstrate it just like Jared did. I've got a lot of socks. But I don't think it would help. They'd just take over, they'd throw us out of the house and bring in a bunch of scientists but then *we'd* never get Mom back. Cause I don't care about studying this thing, I just want to go through it and get Mom."

"Not a chance," said Dad. "If anyone goes, I go."

"Dad," said Todd. "Think about it a minute. If *you* go, then there's no adult here in the house. Just me and Jared. Somebody's going to notice when you don't show up at work. They'll come here and find out you're gone."

"I'll come right back."

"Did *Mom* come right back?" said Todd. "No, because time flows differently there, it's only been a *week* for her, the guy said. So if you're gone even a few hours, that's days and weeks for us. So you're just as stuck as Mom is, and Jared and I are in foster homes somewhere far away from here while the cops try to figure out who murdered you and Mom because there's no chance they'll listen to two crazy kids, right?"

"So there's nothing we can do."

"I can go," said Todd.

"Not a chance," said Dad. "What can you do that I *can't* do?"

"You can cover up my absence," said Todd. "You can say I'm visiting Aunt Heather and Uncle Peace on their hippie commune which doesn't have a phone. You can say it's therapy because I'm still so messed up about Mom's death."

"That still doesn't get you *or* Mom back from… that other place."

"Right," said Todd. "But as long as you're *here*, at the house, you can help us. Because what is Mom's problem? She can't find the mouth on the other side so she can come through it. Eggo knows where it is, he comes through it all the time. So maybe it's in some place where she can't go. Maybe it's inside some building or in a public street where Eggo doesn't want her to be seen. Or maybe he *wants* to keep her captive so he just won't tell her."

"And you think *you* can find it?" asked Dad.

"No," said Todd. "I think you can move it and then show us where it's at."

"Move it?"

"Eggo moved the worm's anus on his side, and it moved the mouth of it into Jared's closet. So if you move the anus on *this* side, the mouth on *that* side should move, too."

"Then neither you nor Mom nor this Eggo person will know where it is," said Dad. "I can't believe I'm talking about moving some interstellar worm's ass."

"It's right out there by the garden hose," said Todd. "You give the thing an enema."

"What?" asked Dad.

"You stick the garden hose in and turn it on full blast."

"What makes you think that will work? It only digests in one direction."

"Eggo threatened to stuff my heart into the anus," said Todd. "You must be able to jam things through that way."

"Unless he was just making a stupid threat that wasn't actually possible."

"Then let's test it," said Todd.

A few minutes later, Dad was in his gym clothes

instead of his pajamas and they stood in the back yard. Todd was afraid that he wouldn't be able to find the spot again, but by standing exactly where he had been when Eggo came through, he could see the very, very slight shimmering in the air. He made both Dad and Jared stand in that spot so they could find it. Then he went and got the garden hose and turned it on, just a trickle, and held the hose up so the water was running back down the green shaft of it.

He took it to the shimmering slice of air and tried to push it through. But it was just like waving it around in the air. It met no resistance, it found no aperture. He was just watering the lawn.

Then he remembered that Jared said you had to approach it from exactly the right angle. He tried to remember which direction Eggo's naked body had come through, and moved so he was standing at exactly the same angle from the hole. Then, very slowly, he extended the hose, holding it just behind the metal end where the water came out.

He felt just a little resistance, just *there*, but when he pushed harder, the hose slid aside and it was just air again.

Exact angle of approach. How much was Eggo's body tilted when it came through?

Todd brought his hand down and pushed the hose upward toward the spot where he had met resistance before. Now it felt solid. Real resistance. "I'm there," he said.

He tried to push the hose in. It went a little way, and to his surprise the water started squirting back at him, like when somebody covers the end of the hose with his thumb.

"Yow!" shouted Jared. "Cool!"

"You got it," said Dad.

"I can't push it through," said Todd. "I'm not strong enough."

"Or it only goes one way," said Jared.

"Help me!" Todd said to Dad.

A moment later, Dad was beside him, gripping Todd's hands over the hose. With his strength added on—or maybe entirely because of his strength, because Todd was certainly no strongman—the end of the hose suddenly moved and...disappeared.

So did the water. Nothing trickled back down the hose. The water was flowing somewhere else.

"Enema," said Jared. "Cool."

Dad let go.

"No!" said Todd. "We've got to move it."

"Where?" said Dad. "How?"

"We've got the hose jammed into it, don't we? Let's use it like a handle and shove it somewhere else."

"Where to?"

"I don't know," said Todd. "I don't think it matters. Eggo couldn't predict where it would move on *our* side, he could only move it where he wanted on *his* side. So let's move it where we want it and let the other side go wherever it goes."

"Maybe thousands of miles."

"What else can we do?" said Todd. "Wherever it is on that side, Dad, Mom hasn't been able to get to it. So we have to move it, and then when I get there, Mom and I have to find it."

"But how?" asked Dad. "If you and Mom are… misty or whatever…"

"Dad," said Todd. "It's probably going to be pretty easy to find. There's water coming out of it."

"Or fog," said Dad. "If things are mistier there."

"Water, fog—*something's* coming out of it right now. So let's move the thing, if we can."

It was only hard because the hose was so flexible. Twice when they tried to move the thing sideways, the hose slipped out, squirting them for a moment before it settled back to being just a trickle. Finally Dad had the idea of using the handle of the rake from the tool shed, and that worked. He shoved it in beside the hose. It was rigid, and they were able to move the thing ten yards across the yard to the shed. The hose slid out as they went, spurting water for a moment when it did.

The shed door was still open, so they easily slid the worm's anus inside.

"Don't pull the rake out yet," said Dad. "Hold it in place."

He ran to the house and came back out with the digital camera. He took pictures of the hose from several angles. "I don't want to run the risk of not being able to get the hose back into it."

It was ten more minutes after that, but Dad got the printouts taped up on the inside walls of the shed. "OK," he said. "Pull out the rake."

It was a lot easier in that direction. *Out* was the direction that the anus wanted things to go.

Dad was all for putting the hose right back in, but Todd said no. "Think about it," said Todd. "I'm not even there yet. And time moves a lot slower there. If we start pumping water, somebody over there is going to notice it. Because it *better* be noticeable in a big way, or Mom and I will never find it."

"They've probably already noticed it," said Dad. "Even that trickle of water wasn't nothing. And what if somebody saw the rake handle?"

"It wasn't all that much water and it wasn't all that long," said Todd. "So give me time to get through and find Mom. Give me time to explain things to her. Eggo said it was hard to talk. Even if it only takes me ten minutes, how long is that *here*, where time goes so much quicker?"

"I see," said Dad. "Can we figure it out?"

"Eggo said maybe it fluctuates. I don't know. We don't want to wait too long, because what if a storm comes up and blows Mom and me to smithereens? So I think maybe...tomorrow? It's a Sunday."

"Too soon," said Jared. "Take your time. What if Mom isn't right there? What if it takes you a long time even to find her?"

"Then when?"

"Next week," said Dad. "A week from now. I can tell the school you're visiting your aunt and uncle, though we'll skip the hippie commune part. And next Saturday morning, we come out and give this thing a full-blast enema."

"Four years," said Jared. "Well, four years and four months. So that's two hundred and...twenty-five weeks. Two-twenty-five to one."

"You're doing all this math in your head?" said Todd. If *Todd* could've done that, he might've been able to become an astronaut.

"Sh," said Jared. "One week is 168 hours. Divide that by 225. That's about three-quarters of an hour. Forty-five minutes."

"I don't think it's that precise," said Todd.

"Even if I'm off by double," said Jared, "that gives you somewhere between twenty minutes and an hour and a half."

"You did that in your head?" asked Dad. "Why do your arithmetic grades suck so badly?"

Jared shrugged. "They make me do all these stupid problems and 'show my work'. What do I put down? 'Think think think'?"

"I don't know if that's enough time," said Todd. "I don't know how long it will take."

"It also means," said Dad, "if we run the water for 225 minutes, it will only be *one* minute on the other side."

"Yeah," said Todd, "but it'll mean that in one minute, 225 minutes worth of water will come through."

"Man," said Jared. "That worm's gonna be doing some serious puking."

"What I'm saying," said Todd, "is that it'll be noticeable."

"And what I'm saying," said Dad, "is that if it takes you half an hour to get to the worm's mouth, we've got to be running that hose for nearly a week."

"Are you worried about the water bill?" said Todd.

"No," said Dad. "Just thinking that in a week, a lot of things might go wrong on our end."

"Dad," said Todd, "so many things can go wrong on both ends that it'll be a miracle if this works at all. But we can't leave Mom there without even trying, can we?"

A few minutes later, Todd was standing in Jared's closet. Stark naked. No point in having his clothes just disappear or whatever they did if you tried to go through the worm wearing them.

"Just make sure you have clothes waiting for Mom and me when we come through in the shed," said Todd.

"You're going to see Mom naked?" said Jared, like it was too weird to imagine.

"It's that or never see her again as long as any of us live," said Todd.

"Mom won't mind," said Dad. "She's in great shape, she kind of likes to show off." He laughed, but it was also kind of a sob.

"Here goes nothing," said Todd.

He reached out his hand.

"Higher," said Jared.

And then the mouth had him. It wasn't like something grabbing him. It was more like getting sucked up against the vacuum cleaner hose. Only instead of sticking to it, he got sucked right in.

He thought he'd come right out the other end, but he didn't. There was time. Like Jonah being stuck in the belly of the whale long enough to call on God to get him out. Only it wasn't a whale, was it, or a big fish, or whatever. It was a worm, like this one. Jonah gets tossed overboard right into the worm's mouth and then it takes him a while to find the mouth on the other side and then he comes through and he's on the beach. He's got to make sense of it somehow, right? So he tells people he was swallowed by a big fish and then God made the fish throw him up on the shore.

That thought took him only a minute. Or a second. Or an hour. And then Todd got distracted by what he was seeing. Stars. All of them distant, but shifting rapidly. As if he were moving through them at an incredible speed. Faster than light. No spaceship around him, no spacesuit, no way to breathe, only he realized that he didn't need to breathe, he could just look and see space all around him until a particular star up ahead didn't move off to the side, it came right at him, getting bigger and brighter, and then he dodged toward a planet and rushed toward the planet's surface, going way too fast, reentry was going to burn him up.

He didn't burn up. He didn't slow down, either. One moment he was plunging toward the planet's surface and the next moment, without any sensation of stopping, he was being squeezed headfirst out of a tight space with waves of peristaltic action. Like a bunch of crap. He could see the ground below him. He couldn't get his arms free. He was going to drop down and land on his face.

And with one last spasm of the worm's colon, that's exactly what happened.

It didn't hurt. He barely felt it. He barely felt anything.

He gathered his legs under him and got his hands in place, like a pushup, only the grassy ground felt like it was hardly there. Or maybe like his fingers weren't there. Then he realized that the bushes around him weren't bushes, they were trees. He was a giant here. A stark naked, insubstantial giant.

He felt a breeze blowing. And on the breeze, a distant voice. Calling his name. "Todd," it was saying. And "no, no," it said.

He looked around, hoping it was Mother, hoping she was off in the distance somewhere. It *was* Mother, but she was not distant. She was entangled in the branches of some trees, not touching the ground at all.

"Hold on, Todd!" she called. It looked like she was shouting with all her strength, but the sound was barely audible. She couldn't be more than twenty feet away. Well, twenty feet compared to their body size—a lot farther compared to the size of the trees.

Hold on, she had said, and now he realized that the breeze was tugging at him, making him drift. He was still in kneeling position, but he was sliding across the ground.

Mother had the right idea, obviously. Get entangled in the branches. Get *caught* so the wind couldn't carry him like a stray balloon.

It took a while to get the knack of it. To move *through* the branches, heedless of how they poked into his skin. It didn't hurt, really. More like tickling sometimes, and sometimes a vague pressure. He figured the tickling was twigs and leaves, the pressure the heavier, more substantial, less-yielding branches.

Carefully, slowly, he made his way among the interlacing branches of the trees until he was close enough to Mother that neither of them had to shout, though their voices were still breathy and soft. "Don't eat anything," she warned him.

"How could I anyway?" he said.

"You can," she said. "And you can drink. But don't do it. It starts to change you. It makes you more solid."

"But isn't that good?"

"We could never go home," said Mother. "That's what *he* says, anyway. If I ever want to get home, I can't eat or drink."

"You haven't eaten or drunk anything in a week?" asked Todd.

"What are you doing here?" she said. "Why did you come through the hole in the closet?"

"Why did *you*?" he said. "Jared warned you."

"How could I believe him?" She started to cry. "Now we're both trapped here."

"Mom," said Todd. "Two things. First, we have a plan. Dad and Jared are going to help us find the worm's mouth."

"Worm's mouth?" she asked.

"And the second thing. It's been four years."

"No," she said. "A week. It's been a week."

"Four years," repeated Todd. "Look at me. I'm older. I'm bigger. Jared is, too. Four years we thought you were dead."

"A week," she murmured. "Oh, my poor children. My poor husband."

"Mom, you've got to be thirsty. You can't last a week without any water."

"I don't get as thirsty as I thought I would. But yes, I'm getting very weak now. I expected— I thought that pretty soon I'll just let go and blow away."

"Don't let go," said Todd. "Just hold on until they turn on the hose." Then he told her about the plan.

It was the longest week of Jared's life. He kept wanting to go out and check the worm's butt to make sure it was there in the shed. Or sit and stare at the mouth in the closet. But he knew if he did that, he'd start wanting to throw things in it. Or go through it himself so he could see Mom. It wasn't fair that Todd got to see her first, when Jared was the one who knew about it all along. But I saw her last, Jared told himself. That wasn't fair either. And if I accidentally or on purpose go through the mouth, who'll help Dad? Who'll turn the hose on?

Who'll keep watch in case the elf comes back?

Because what Jared knew about the elf was this: He wasn't nice. He didn't want Mom to come back. Hadn't Jared begged him to bring her back, the first time he saw him after Mom went through? And the elf just shoved him away. It hurt so bad. The elf was so *strong*.

What if the elf came back and went through the mouth and saw Todd and Mom and realized what was happening and…and *killed* them? He might. He was selfish and cruel, Jared knew that about him. He didn't care about anybody. Oh, he asked questions, all the time, but he never answered any, he wouldn't tell anything. "You wouldn't understand anyway, you're just a child," he said. Well, children understand things, Jared wanted to scream at him. But he never did. Because if he got too demanding, if he got *mad*, the elf just left. And what if the elf shoved him again? He didn't want the elf to shove him. It hurt, deep inside, when he did that.

So Jared went through the days with Dad. Without Todd there, Jared and Dad had to do all kinds of jobs. He hadn't realized how hard Todd worked, all the things he did. Or how lonely it got without Todd there to gripe at and play with and yell at and fight over the television remote with.

He had thought all these years that it would be so nice if anyone would just believe him. But he hadn't thought through what that might mean. Believe him and then what? Well, then they would *do* something about it. But he thought it would be like the government would do it, the police, the fire department. Somebody official who already knew all about everything and they could just say, Oh, lost your mother in one of *those* things, of course, happens all the time, give us a minute...there! There's your mom!

But of course it couldn't work that way. Nobody knew anything about this. Nobody could just fix it. They had to do it themselves. So now the question was: Would Mom come back? Or had they just lost Todd, too? And if Todd couldn't come back, either, would the cops think Dad had killed him and Mom both and lock him up and put Jared in foster care? A part of him wished they had just left things alone. Losing Mom was bad. But losing everybody else, too, wouldn't exactly make anything better. If he had just kept it to himself. If he had just refused to put that sock into the monster's mouth when Todd told him to.

If…

Then it would be Jared's fault if Mom never came back. Even thinking like this, wasn't that the same as wishing Mom would never come home? I'm selfish and evil, Jared thought. I don't even deserve to have a mother.

And then, underneath all the wondering and worrying and blaming, there was this, like a constant drumbeat: Hope. Mom was coming home. Todd would get her and Jared and Dad would show them where the mouth was on the other side by hosing the worm's butt, and they'd all be together again and it would be partly because Jared knew and showed them and helped make it happen.

He nearly flunked three different tests that week and the teachers were quite concerned at his sudden lapse in performance. It was hard to concentrate on anything. Hard to think that their stupid baby easy meaningless tests were worth taking. Hard even to listen to their sympathetic blabbing. "Is everything all right at home?" My brother just got swallowed up by the same monster that ate my mom, but we've got a plan, so, "Everything's fine." "Has anyone *done* anything to you?" Jared knew what they were asking, but apart from the worm in the closet eating his mom and his brother, Jared had to say that nobody had done anything to *him* at all.

And then it was Friday and he got to go home from school and fix himself some food and stay away from the closet because that would make him crazy, to sit and stare at the thing. Nothing was ever coming out of it, and nobody except the stupid elf was ever going into it again. There was nothing to see.

Except there he was when Dad got home, the closet door open and Jared sitting on the floor just looking at it, remembering Mom's look of panic as the thing caught hold of her and then how she looked, just her left shoulder and the rest of her body still in the closet, but not her head, not her right shoulder or arm, because they were going, and how Jared lunged and caught her but then she was torn right out of his arms. Like the thing had to get her in two swallows.

In two *bites*.

"Whatcha lookin' at?" Dad asked. Softly, which meant he didn't think anything was really funny.

"It didn't take Mom all at once," said Jared. "What if it bit her in half? What if she's dead and Todd can't ever bring her home?"

Dad took a slow breath. "Then Todd will tell us that when he gets back."

"And if he never comes back?"

"Then we'll move away from here."

"And leave somebody else to find it?"

"Jared, what can we do? Nuke the house? We didn't make this problem. Especially not you. It was done *to* us. And we're doing our best to undo it." He came and sat beside Jared. "Things can get a lot worse. Or they can get a lot better. But at least we're doing something, and we're doing the best thing we could think of, and what more can anybody do?"

Jared didn't answer. There wasn't an answer.

"Let's have dinner and watch a DVD tonight," said Dad. "What about a Harry Potter movie? What about all of them?"

"No magic," said Jared, shuddering in spite of himself. "No crap about people turning invisible or going back in time or three-headed dogs or vines that choke you or chessmen that try to kill you or teachers with a face on the back of their head."

"*Charlotte's Web?*"

"Dad, that's for kids."

So they watched *The Dirty Dozen* and when they threw those grenades down the shafts and the German officers in the bomb shelter were panicking and screaming, Jared felt a moment of breathless panic himself, but then he thought: At least the good guys were *doing* something, even though some of them were going to get killed in the process, even though some of them would never get home.

They were saving the world, maybe. Or helping to. We're just saving Mom.

But to Jared, that was better than saving the world. He didn't care about the world.

Saturday morning, Jared was up before the sun. He wanted to wake Dad, but he waited. And not long. Dad usually slept in on Saturday, but today he joined Jared at the breakfast table, pouring out Cheerios and stirring a couple of spoonfuls of brown sugar into the bowl and eating them, all without milk.

"That's so gross," said Jared.

"Better than watching the milk turn grey with sugar," said Dad.

"Do we have to wait till, like, noon or something?" asked Jared.

"There's a lot of oat bran in this stuff," said Dad. "I think I'll need to use the bathroom before I can go anywhere or do anything."

"Yeah, and you'll read a whole book in there."

"Reading, the best laxative." Dad said it in his Lee Marvin voice, which was a pretty good imitation.

"You might as well stick a plug in it," said Jared. "When you're reading, you never let fly."

"I can't believe you're speaking of the bodily functions of your father." This time Dad was doing Charles Bronson. It was nothing like Charles Bronson, actually, but somehow Jared knew that was who he was doing.

"We're giving an interstellar worm an enema today, Dad. I got rectums on my mind."

And Dad went into Groucho Marx. "I don't let anybody say my kid's got poop for brains."

"Poop?" said Jared.

"Got to get used to saying 'poop,' now that Mom's coming back."

"Is she, Dad?"

Dad's Groucho-Marx grin didn't fade, but his voice came out like W.C. Fields. "I'll never lie to you, my boy. Now finish your breakfast, you bother me."

"That's all you got? Lee Marvin, a half-assed Charles Bronson, Groucho Marx, and W.C. Fields?"

"I did three others that you didn't catch," said Dad. "And besides, I had Cheerios in my mouth."

"Oh!" said Jared, doing the old family joke associated with Cheerios. "O-o-o-o-oh."

Which would have been the cue for Dad to launch into singing "We're off to see the wizard, the wonderful Wizard of Oh's," but instead he reached across the table and covered Jared's hand with his own. "I can't really eat much this morning, can you?"

"You see anything in my mouth?" said Jared.

Dad pushed back from the table. "I've gotta see a man about a hose."

Jared followed him out into the back yard. Dad unlocked the back shed and set down the clothes he had brought for Todd and Mom, while Jared unspooled the hose and dragged it across the lawn. Of course it got heavier the farther he pulled it, but it didn't slow him down. Quite the contrary—by the time he reached the shed, he was running.

"Careful," said Dad. "Let's do this methodically and get it right."

Jared watched as Dad found the gap in the air, following the pictures taped to the wall. Then he pushed it in, and kept pushing, and pushing. "Get me more slack, Jared."

Jared went back to the hose reel and pulled it until it was stretched tight. He could see Dad back in the shed, pushing more and more of it into the hole in the air, so it looked for all the world as if it were disappearing.

"It's pushing back," said Dad. "It wants to get it out."

"Wouldn't *you?*" asked Jared.

"Turn the water on. Full blast. Every bit of pressure the city can give us."

Jared turned the handle, turned and turned until it couldn't open any more. He could see Dad bracing his back against the shelves, pushing forward against the worm's efforts to expel the enema.

Jared walked closer to the shed, to ask whether any water was coming back or whether it was all getting through, when he saw the elf walking toward him across the back lawn.

Careful not to speed up, Jared continued toward the shed, but instead of talking or even letting himself look at what Dad was doing, he closed the door, loudly saying as he did so, "Hello, Eggo. Why didn't you tell me that was your name?" With any luck, Dad would realize that they didn't exactly want the elf to know what they were doing.

"You never asked," said Eggo. He headed toward the sideyard fence beyond where the worm's anus used to be and started stripping off his clothes in order to stow them back in the box. Only when he was down to his pants did he turn around and look at Jared, who was now leaning against the corner of the house, looking as nonchalant as he could.

"What are you watching?" he asked.

"All these years I see you, you never tell me anything. One time you talk to Todd, and suddenly you're full of information."

"You were a baby."

"I was, but I'm not now."

"So...what do you want to know?" Eggo returned to stripping off his pants. He was buck naked now, stuffing everything into a plastic bag before putting it into the box.

"When are you going to get Mom back to us?"

"I didn't take your mommy away from you," said Eggo. "It's none of my business."

"You're like half a worm," said Jared. "All asshole, no heart."

Eggo reburied the box and stood back up. By Jared's rough guess, it had been about five minutes since he started the water running. That was three hundred seconds. So in the other place, it wouldn't even have been running for two full seconds yet.

Eggo was looking at him. "What are you doing?"

"Math in my head," said Jared.

"I mean with the hose. The water's on, I can hear it, but you've got it flowing into the shed."

"Through the shed and out the back window," said Jared. "It's the only way to reach the very back of the yard without buying a longer hose."

But Eggo wasn't buying it. He was striding toward the shed now.

"It's none of your business!" cried Jared. "Haven't you done enough? Why don't you leave us alone!"

Eggo turned back to face Jared. "Everything's my business if I decide it is," he said. "What are you hiding in there?"

The elf glanced toward the place where there had once been a shimmering slit in the air. He walked toward it, searching. He waved his hand. "What have you done?" he said. He whirled and faced Jared. "You moved it, you little moron! Do you know what you've done? I'll never find it! It'll take months!"

"Good!" shouted Jared. "I hope it takes you *years*, because that'll be *centuries* here, and I won't ever have to see your ugly face and your ugly butt again!"

The elf's face was turning red as he strode toward Jared. His hand rose up as if to smack at him—to swat him into oblivion, as if he were a fly. But then the elf looked at the hose again and then at the shed and then he took off running straight toward it.

"Dad!" shouted Jared. "Don't try to fight him! He'll kill you!"

Eggo flung the door of the shed open—flung it so hard that it ripped from the hinges and sailed like a frisbee halfway across the lawn. Jared saw that Dad must have understood what was happening, because instead of holding on to the hose, he was gripping the chain saw and pulling the cord. It roared to life just as Eggo reached for the hose.

"Just how dense do you think you are!" shouted Dad.

Eggo backed off a little, but he was holding the hose now, pulling it out. "You moved it! You can't move it!"

"We already did," yelled Jared, "and you'll never

get it back exactly where it was!"

"You're drowning my city!" shouted the elf.

"You kept my mother there when you could have brought her home!"

By now Dad had stepped out of the shed and was approaching Eggo. "Drop the hose!" he yelled. "I don't want to see how much damage this can do!"

Eggo roared and smacked at the chainsaw with his left hand. It flew out of Dad's grasp, staggering him; but the elf came away from the encounter with his hand bleeding. No, spurting blood.

The deadman switch on the chainsaw shut it down, now that nobody was gripping the handle. The sudden silence was deafening.

"What have you done to me!" wailed Eggo.

"You want me to call 911?" asked Jared.

"Drop the hose," said Dad.

"I'll bleed to death!"

"Drop the hose." Dad was picking up the chainsaw again.

Eggo stamped his left foot repeatedly, spinning him in a circle as he howled and gripped his bleeding hand. It was as if he was screwing his right foot into the ground, and indeed it was already in the lawn up to the knee.

"You *are* Rumpelstiltskin, you little jerk," Jared said. "You told Todd that you weren't!"

"We're going to get them home, and you're not going to stop us," said Dad. The chainsaw roared to life.

With a final howl, Eggo pulled his right foot out of the ground and ran into the house. Not through any of the doors—he leapt for the wall and his body hurtled through, leaving torn vinyl siding and broken studs and peeled-back drywall behind him. Jared ran to the gap in the wall in time to see Eggo dive through the worm's mouth.

He turned around to see Dad already back at the shed, pushing the hose back up into the worm's anus.

"What if he hurts them?" asked Jared. "He's gone back and he'll find them."

"We can only hope they're already on their way."

"The water only started a couple of seconds ago, in that world."

"Then I hope they aren't wasting any time," said Dad. "What else can we do?"

Once Mom understood what Todd was talking about, he began to ask her questions. She didn't know any answers. "If I try to go anywhere, either the wind starts lifting me or people see me and start throwing rocks or…screaming, or calling for other people to come and look and…I'm naked."

Todd knew perfectly well she was naked. But to his surprise, it didn't *feel* like she was naked. She was so misty that it was as if she were wearing the leaves behind her—he saw them better than he saw her.

"But you have to know where he comes from."

"He comes from the same hole in the air that we came through," said Mom.

"Then where does he *go*?"

"How can I tell, from here in the leaves?"

"I mean where does he *head*? Which way? Uphill? Downhill?"

"I'm sorry," she said. "Downhill. I just didn't—I can't think. It's like my mind is fading along with my body. I think bits of me have been blowing away. I'm being shredded. I'm leaving pieces of me in the tree. Todd, I don't even know if I *can* go home. Maybe if I get back there I'll die."

"You'll have a better chance there than here. Can you hold my hand?"

"I can't hold anything," she said.

But when he held out his hand to her, she took it. And he felt her hand in his. He could hold on to her. Better than he could hold on to the branches, because she wasn't so hard and unyielding; he didn't feel as if his body would tear itself apart if he held her too tightly. "Stay with me," he said. "We'll try to get closer to the mouth of the worm. If *he* goes this way, the mouth has got to be down here, too."

The faster they moved, the more control they had, or so it felt. Their feet touched the ground very lightly, but they didn't bounce up and into the air. With the wind coming from their right side, they had to keep correcting in order to move in the direction they intended. But soon enough they emerged from the trees and there was a town.

It looked vaguely oriental, mostly because of the shape of the roofs on the nearest houses. The colors of the walls had once been garish, but they were faded, the paint peeling. But there wasn't time to study the architecture. People were milling around in the streets, jabbering at each other. They didn't speak a language Todd had ever heard before. How could they? Only Eggo had had a chance to learn English. There'd be no talking with these people. No asking them for directions.

Then again, maybe it wouldn't be necessary. Because now he could see what they were all excited about. The street was covered with a drift of water. Not puddles, a drift—thicker than a mist or a fog, but not rushing anywhere, just hovering.

It was the trickle of water they had sent through the hose when they first tested it up the worm's anus. Only here, it was a lot of water.

Which meant that the original position of the worm's mouth wasn't far from here.

"Come on," he said to Mom, dragging her around the crowd.

"Wait," she said. "It's water from *our* world, isn't it? Todd, I'm so thirsty."

He couldn't force her to stay with him, though he thought it was a bad idea for her to head toward the people. He needn't have worried, though. They were apparently so freaked out by the water that it made them jumpy. When Mom started drifting through the crowd, they parted for her, and some of them screamed and ran away. She knelt in the pool of water and drank.

Todd could watch her gain solidity as she did. Apparently the lack of water had desiccated her, faded her. Now she was more solid, and more naked,

but still it didn't bother him. It was like seeing a baby naked. There was a job to do, no time to worry about embarrassment.

He drifted toward her; but the moment he touched the water, it felt familiar and real—and cold and wet. He slogged through the water to where she knelt. "Let's go now, Mom, before they start figuring out just how solid we aren't."

She drank just a little more, then took his hand. They made better progress now that she could find a little better purchase for her feet, more strength in her legs. At the same time, being more solid made her more vulnerable to the wind.

They found the source of the water—a house. The people had broken down the door, apparently to find out what was causing the mini-flood, or perhaps to make sure no one was inside, drowning.

Todd also saw that the water trailed off in another direction. "When we moved it, the hose stayed with it for a few steps. I think the new location must be in that direction."

He pulled her along. She stopped and drank again. "I need that water," she said. "Don't leave it behind."

"There's plenty of water where we're going," he said.

"But you don't *know* where we're going. Just…this direction."

"Mom, we only took a few steps before the hose fell out, and here it's hundreds of yards. So the final location could be a mile farther on. We've got to keep moving."

A crowd of people, many of them children, were following them as they drifted out of the water and on up the streets. Todd tried to figure what a straight line would be, extending in the direction that the thick low fog had trailed off, but the streets weren't cooperating. He kept trying to double back to get in the line, but nothing led in the right direction.

Until finally they reached a street with a high fence enclosing a park, with green lawns and stately trees. He wasn't sure exactly where the line from the hosewater would have intersected with the park, but he knew it was bound to reach it somewhere. Quite possibly the real flood, when it came, would pour out in this park, which would make it much easier to see.

As if on command, there was a loud crashing sound not very far off, and when Todd looked in that direction, he saw a wall of water rushing toward them—toward the whole length of the fence.

There was no point in trying to face it head-on.

They had to get around the flood, behind it. And for now, the only way to do that without having to slog through water was to get above it.

He led his mother up into one of the trees. But in this wide open park, they couldn't climb hand over hand, tree to tree. There were wide gaps, and all they could do was leap, hoping they wouldn't get taken by the wind and drift away.

It was slow going, but they made steady progress, and Todd did a fair job of estimating how the breeze would influence their flight. It was kind of exhilarating, to leap out into the air and drift only slowly downward, over the rushing water.

And as they moved around the water, they found that it was flowing out of a huge house. The crashing sound had been the stone front wall of the house giving way, crumbling from the pressure of the thick fog. Which seemed absurd. Except that the water would be coming so hard and fast out of the hose on this end that it wasn't *water* pressure that knocked down the wall, it was the explosive force of air pressure.

He heard shouting behind him, which wasn't a surprise; but it was growing closer, which was. Most of the people had fled from the flood when they saw it coming at them through the wrought-iron fence. But now there was someone plunging ahead through the water. It was easier for him than it would have been for Todd or Mom—the water was only fog to him, though it was a very thick one.

It was Eggo. And he was aiming something at them.

A gun. He had a gun.

Eggo fired. The bullet passed through Todd. He felt it, but not as pain. More like a belch, a rumbling. But that didn't mean the damage wasn't real.

"Why are you doing this!" shouted Todd.

He could see that Eggo didn't hear him. "Keep going toward that house, Mother." He let go of her hand. "Go! Don't make all this a wasted effort!"

She went, looking at him once in anguish but plunging ahead.

Todd headed straight toward Eggo, who was re-loading the thing. It was a muzzle-loader. He only had a musket. Thank heaven he hadn't figured out how to make an AK-47.

"Don't be stupid!" shouted Todd. "Stop it!"

Now the elf heard him. "No!" he shouted. "You wrecked everything!"

"The sooner we get back home, the sooner this flood will stop!"

"I don't care!" shouted Eggo. "That's the king's house, you fool! You destroyed the king's house!"

"And you can save it by driving us out of here! Let us go, and be the hero who ended the flood!"

Eggo's gun was loaded and he was pointing it right at Todd, who was close enough now that he thought this time it would probably hurt.

But Eggo didn't fire the thing. "All right!" he said. "Go! I'll shoot *past* you. Just get out of here. And act like you're afraid of me!"

"I won't be acting," murmured Todd.

But he couldn't change direction in mid-air, and he knew if he once got into that water, he'd never be able to take off again.

"Give me a push!" he shouted at Eggo.

Eggo ran at him and held up the barrel of his musket. Todd grabbed it, barely clung to it with his attenuated fingers, and then hung on for dear life as the elf swung him and threw him toward the palace, where Mom was just reaching the huge gap through which water was flowing.

Soon they were inside, grabbing sconces and chandeliers and furniture to keep them moving forward through the air over the flood. And finally they found it, the place where a huge, thick hose-end was spewing out an incredible volume of icy, jet-speed water. Todd made the mistake of being in the path of the blast and it felt like it had broken half his ribs. He dropped down into the water. Mom screamed and pulled herself down to help him, which saved *her* from getting blasted by another whiplike pass from the hose.

"We've got to get under it," he said. "Look for where the hose comes out of nothing. We have to climb the hose into the worm's mouth!"

Now it was Mom's turn to drag Todd, through the water, barely raising their heads above the surface to breathe. Finally they got behind the hose-end, and even though it was whipping around, the base of it, the place where it came out of nowhere, was fairly solidly in place.

The hose was exactly the right size for Todd to grip it. "You first!" he shouted to Mom. "Climb up the hose! When you get to the end, tell them to turn it off, but don't pull it out till I climb down after you!"

Mom gripped the hose and when her hand inched up past the place where the hose disappeared, it also vanished. "Keep climbing," Todd urged her. "Don't stop no matter what you see. Don't let go!"

As Mom disappeared, he turned around to avoid watching her, and to take one last look around the room. There were soldiers in flamboyantly colored uniforms gathered in the doorways, aiming arrows at him. Oh, good, he thought. They don't have guns.

The chainsaw lay discarded on the lawn. Jared stood near it, straddling the hose, watching as Dad wrestled with it like a python. He couldn't keep it from being thrust back at him, no matter how tightly he held it against the spot where it became invisible. Suddenly a loop of it would extrude and Dad would have to grasp it again, at the new endpoint. Already several coils were on the floor. What if Mom and Todd weren't anywhere near the point where it emerged on the other side? What if all of this was for nothing?

And then, along with a coil of hose, a hand emerged out of nothingness in the shed.

Dad let go of the hose and took the hand, dragged at it.

Mother's head emerged from the wormhole.

"Turn off the water!" she croaked. "Turn it off, but keep the hose—"

Jared was already rushing for the faucet. He turned it off, turned back to face her, and...

The hose lay completely on the ground, Mom tangled up in it. Nothing was poking into the worm's anus now. How would Todd get back?

Mom and Dad were hugging while at the same time Dad was trying to wrap a shirt around her, to cover her.

"What about Todd!" Jared shouted.

"He's coming," said Mom. "He's right behind me."

"The hose is out of the worm!"

Apparently they hadn't realized it until now. Father lunged for the hose end, still dripping, and tried frantically to reinsert it. Mother, half-wearing the shirt now, tried to help him, but she was panting heavily and then she collapsed onto the hose.

Dad cried out and dropped the hose-end. "He's right behind me," Mom whispered.

Jared helped him get Mom up. She wasn't un-conscious; once Dad was holding her, she could shuffle along. Dad led her toward the house.

Jared took up the hose again and started trying to

feed it through. Finding the hole was hard; pushing the hose was harder.

Until he realized: It doesn't have to be the hose anymore. We aren't trying to pump water any more.

He found the rake and fed the handle of it into the gap in the air. Rigid, the handle went in much more easily—which was to say, it took all of Jared's strength, but he could do it. He jammed the handle in all the way up to the metal of the rake and then held it there, gripping it tightly and bracing his feet against the lowest shelf on the wall of the shed.

The rake kept lunging toward him, pressing at him, shoving him backward, but he'd push it in again. It went on until he was too tired to hold it any longer and his belly and hips hurt where the rake had jabbed him, but still he held.

And then a hand came out of the hole along with a shove of the rake, and this time Jared shoved back only long enough to get out from behind the rake. It was practically shot out of the wormhole, and along with it came Todd.

Todd was bleeding all over from vicious-looking puncture wounds. "They shot me," he said, and then he fell into unconsciousness.

Mother spent two days in the hospital, rehydrating and recovering. They pumped her with questions about what had happened, where she was for four years and four months, but she told them over and over that she couldn't remember, that one minute she was putting Jared to bed, and the next minute she was lying out in the shed, gasping for breath, feeling as if someone had stretched her so thin that a gust of wind could blow her away.

They questioned Jared, too. And Dad. What did you see? How did you find them? Did you see who hurt your brother? And all they could say, either of them, was, "Mom was just there in the shed. And after we helped her back into the house, we came out and Todd was there, too, bleeding, and we called 911."

Because Dad had told Mom and Jared, "No lies. Tell the truth. Up to Mom going and after Mom and Todd reappeared. No explanations. No guesses. Nothing. We don't know anything, we don't remember anything."

Jared didn't bother telling him that "I don't remember" was a huge lie. He knew enough to realize that telling the truth would convince everybody that they were liars, and only lies would convince anybody they were telling the truth.

Todd didn't recover consciousness after the surgery for three days, and then he was in and out as his body fought off a devastating fever and an infection that antibiotics didn't seem to help. So delirious that nothing he said made sense—to the cops and the doctors, anyway. Men with arrows. Elves. Eggo waffles. Worms with mouths and anuses. Flying through space. Floods and flying and...definitely delirium.

The cops found what looked like bloodstains on the chainsaw, but since Todd's wounds were punctures and the stains turned out not to react properly to any of the tests for blood, the evidence led them nowhere. It might end up in somebody's X file, but what the whole event would not do is end up in court.

When Todd woke up for real, Dad and Jared were there by his bed. Dad only had time to say, "It's a shame if you don't remember anything at all," before the detective and the doctor were both all over him, asking how it happened, who did it, where the injuries were inflicted.

"On another planet," said Todd. "I flew through space to get there and I never let go of the hose but then it got sucked away from me and I was lost until I got jabbed in the shoulder with the rake and I held on and rode it home."

That was even better than amnesia, since the doctor assumed he was still delirious and they left Todd and Dad and Jared alone. Later, when Todd was clearly *not* delirious, he was ready with his own amnesia story, along with tales of weird dreams he had while in a coma.

The doctor's report finally said that Todd's injuries were consistent with old-fashioned arrows, the kind with barbs, only there were no removal injuries. It was as if the arrows had entered his body and dissolved somehow. And as to where Mom had been all those years, they hadn't a clue, and except for dehydration and some serious but generalized weight loss, she seemed to be in good health.

And when at last they were home together, they didn't talk about it much. One time through the story so everybody would know what happened to everybody else, but then it was done.

Mom couldn't get over how many years she had missed, how much bigger and older Todd and Jared had become. She started blaming herself for being gone that whole time, but Dad wouldn't let her. "We all did what made sense to us at the time," he said. "The best we could. And we're back together *now*. Todd has some interesting scars. You have to take calcium pills to recover from bone loss. There's only one thing left to take care of."

The mouth of the worm in the closet. The anus of the worm in the shed.

The solution wasn't elegant, but it worked. First they hooked the anus with the rake one last time, covered the top with a tarpaulin, and dragged it to the car. They drove to the lake and dragged the thing up to the edge of a steep cliff overlooking the water, then shoved it as far as they could over the edge, with Dad and Mom gripping Todd tightly so he wouldn't fall.

Let Eggo come back if he wanted. Given how tough he was, it probably wouldn't hurt him much, but it would be a very inconvenient location.

The mouth in the closet was harder, because they couldn't move it from their end. But a truckload of manure dumped on the front lawn allowed them to bring wheelbarrows full of it into the house and on into the bedroom, where they took turns shoveling it into the maw.

On the other side, they knew, it would be a fine mist of manure, spreading with the wind out across the town. Huge volumes of it, coming thick and fast.

And sure enough, by the time the manure pile was half gone, the mouth disappeared. Eggo must have moved it from his end. Which was all they wanted.

Of course, then they had to get the smell out of the house and spread a huge amount of leftover manure over the lawn and across the garden, and the neighbors were really annoyed with the stench in the neighborhood until a couple of rains had settled it down. But they had a great lawn the next spring.

Only one thing that Todd had to know. He asked Mom when they were alone one night, watching the last installment of the BBC miniseries of *Pride and Prejudice* after Dad and Jared had fallen asleep.

"What did you see?" he asked. "During the passage?" When she seemed baffled, he added, "Between worlds."

"See?" asked Mom. "What did *you* see?"

"It was like I was in space," said Todd, "only I could breathe. Faster than light I was going, stars everywhere, and then I zoomed down to the planet and…there I was."

She shook her head. "I guess we each saw what we wanted to see. Needed to see, maybe. No outer space for me. No stars. Just you and Jared and your dad, waiting for me. Beckoning to me. Telling me to come home."

"And the hose?"

"Never saw it," she said. "During the whole passage. I could *feel* it, hold tightly to it, but all I saw was…home."

Todd nodded. "OK," he said. "But it *was* another planet, just the same. Even if I didn't really see my passage through space. It was a real place, and I was there."

"You were there," said Mom.

"And you know what?" said Todd.

"I hope you're not telling me you ever want to go back."

"Are you kidding?" said Todd. "I've had my fill of space travel. I'm done."

"There's no place like home," said Mom, clicking her heels together.